LITTLE TURTLE TRIES

by MICHAEL DAHL   ILLUSTRATED BY ORIOL VIDAL

Oh Little Turtle!
It's time to get dressed!

Oops!
Try again, Little Turtle.

That's a bit better.
But something is still
not quite right . . .

Oops!

Keep trying, Little Turtle!

You are so close!

Almost there . . .

Way to go, Little Turtle!

You kept trying,
and you did it!

But now it's time to get UNdressed.

Grab your pjs, Little Turtle!
It's time for bed.

Hello Genius is published by Capstone Editions, a Capstone imprint
1710 Roe Crest Drive, North Mankato, Minnesota 56003
capstonepub.com

Copyright © 2021 by Capstone

Library of Congress Cataloging-in-Publication data
is available on the Library of Congress website.

ISBN: 9781684468423 (paperback)

Printed and bound in China. PO5700

hello genius

written by
Michael Dahl

illustrated by
Oriol Vidal

LITTLE ELEPHANT LISTENS

hello genius™

LITTLE ELEPHANT LISTENS

written by
Michael Dahl

illustrated by
Oriol Vidal

Little Elephant uses his BIG ears to listen.

He listens to Papa Elephant.

He listens to Brother Elephant.

He listens to Mama Elephant.

He listens to Papa and Mama Elephant.

"Time for bed!"

ZZZZZzzZZZzZ

And at bedtime everyone else listens...

...to Little Elephant!

ZZZZZZZzz

Hello Genius is published by Picture Window Books, a Capstone imprint
1710 Roe Crest Drive, North Mankato, Minnesota 56003
capstonepub.com

Copyright © 2014 by Picture Window Books

Library of Congress Cataloging-in-Publication data
is available on the Library of Congress website.

ISBN: 9781484688021 (paperback)

Printed and bound in China.   PO5700

hello genius™

LITTLE TIGER PICKS UP

written by
Michael Dahl

illustrated by
Oriol Vidal

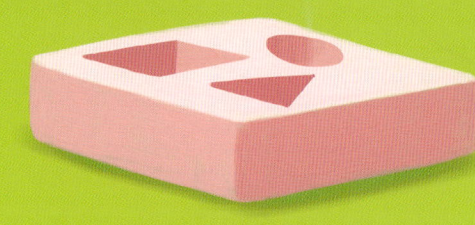

Oh my! What a mess, Little Tiger!

"ROAR!"

Playtime is over.

It's time to pick up.

Pick up your toys,
Little Tiger.

Pick up your games, Little Tiger.

Pick up your books, Little Tiger.

"Everything is picked up," says Little Tiger.

Good job, Little Tiger!

Now it is time

to pick YOU up!

"ROAR!"

Hello Genius is published by Picture Window Books, a Capstone imprint
1710 Roe Crest Drive, North Mankato, Minnesota 56003
capstonepub.com

Copyright © 2014 by Picture Window Books

Library of Congress Cataloging-in-Publication data
is available on the Library of Congress website.

ISBN: 9781484688038 (paperback)

Printed and bound in China. PO5700

NO WORRIES FOR WHALE

by MICHAEL DAHL
ILLUSTRATED BY ORIOL VIDAL

What's wrong, Little Whale?

I'm worried.

Where's my food?

I'll help you find food,
Little Whale.

No worries.

What's wrong, Little Whale?

I'm worried.

Who will play with me?

We'll all play together,
Little Whale.

No worries.

Now what's wrong, Little Whale?

I'm worried.

Who will take care of me when it's dark?

I'll take care of you,
Little Whale.

When it's dark,
we'll snuggle and sleep.

No worries, Little Whale.

I'm always here.

Hello Genius is published by Capstone Editions, a Capstone imprint
1710 Roe Crest Drive, North Mankato, Minnesota 56003
capstonepub.com

Copyright © 2021 by Capstone

Library of Congress Cataloging-in-Publication data
is available on the Library of Congress website.

ISBN: 9781684468430 (paperback)

Printed and bound in China. PO5700

hello genius™

JUST BREATHE, BEAR

BY CHRISTIANNE JONES   ILLUSTRATED BY ORIOL VIDAL

Bear is worried.

Just breathe, Bear.

In, in, in,

and

out, out, out.

Bear is sad.

Just breathe, Bear.

In, in, in,
and
out, out, out.

Bear is angry.

Just breathe, Bear.

In, in, in,

and

out, out, out.

Bear is scared.

Just breathe, Bear.

In, in, in,

and

out, out, out.

Bear is loved.

Just smile, Bear.

You are going to be okay.

Hello Genius is published by Capstone Editions, a Capstone imprint
1710 Roe Crest Drive, North Mankato, Minnesota 56003
capstonepub.com

Copyright © 2022 by Capstone

Library of Congress Cataloging-in-Publication data
is available on the Library of Congress website.

ISBN: 9781684468447 (paperback)

Printed and bound in China. PO5700

hello genius™

GO TO BED, GOAT

BY MICHAEL DAHL   ILLUSTRATED BY ORIOL VIDAL

It's bedtime, Goat.
Please put on
your pajamas.

Silly Goat!

It's bedtime, Goat.
Please brush your teeth.

Silly Goat!

It's bedtime, Goat.
Please use the potty.

Silly Goat!

It's bedtime, Goat.
No more sillies.

Lie down nice and quiet.

Snuggle under your blanket, calm your body, and close your eyes.

I love you,

silly Goat!

Good night!

Hello Genius is published by Capstone Editions, a Capstone imprint
1710 Roe Crest Drive, North Mankato, Minnesota 56003
capstonepub.com

Copyright © 2020 by Capstone

Library of Congress Cataloging-in-Publication data
is available on the Library of Congress website.

ISBN: 9781684468454 (paperback)

Printed and bound in China. PO5700